PALACE OF DECEPTION

When a Mediterranean princess disappears with just weeks to go before her investiture, Lizzie Smith takes on the acting role of her life — she is to impersonate Princess Charlotte so that the ceremony can go ahead. As Lizzie immerses herself in preparation, her only confidante is Léon, her quiet bodyguard. In the glamorous setting of the Palace of Montverrier, Lizzie begins to fall for Léon. But what secrets is he keeping from her? And who can she really trust?

Books by Helena Fairfax
in the Linford Romance Library:

THE SILK ROMANCE
THE ANTIQUE LOVE

HELENA FAIRFAX

PALACE OF DECEPTION

Complete and Unabridged

LINFORD
Leicester

First published in Great Britain in 2015

First Linford Edition
published 2017

A catalogue record for this book is available
from the British Library.

ISBN 978–1–4448–3183–2

Published by
F. A. Thorpe (Publishing)
Anstey, Leicestershire

Set by Words & Graphics Ltd.
Anstey, Leicestershire
Printed and bound in Great Britain by
T. J. International Ltd., Padstow, Cornwall

This book is printed on acid-free paper

To Joe
Wish you were here

1

The tiny country of Montverrier is a secret jewel, hidden away in southern Europe, between the mountains and the Mediterranean. It has no airport, and so Mr Ross had provided me with first-class tickets to travel by train; a winding journey along the coast road, past fields of sunflowers on one side, and the glittering Mediterranean on the other. As the high speed train glided further south, the unease that had dogged me since leaving Edinburgh began to melt away, warmed by the sun and the vibrant colours. I pressed my face to the window and gazed out at the horizon, where the burnt orange of the sunflowers merged with a brilliant blue sky. All was as still as an oil painting. How could anything sinister ever happen in such a glorious place?

By the time I stepped onto the gleaming concourse at Montverrier station, my misgivings had almost entirely lifted. The sun's rays filtered through the great glass roof and onto the tiled floor. Through the open doors I could see the distinctive trunks of palm trees and, best of all, the sea, with the light dancing on its waves in blue and silver. A wonderful heat seeped into my damp Scottish bones, and for a moment I stood there, revelling in the warmth of it. I would have loved nothing better than to set off exploring, but, mindful of my instructions to keep myself out of the public gaze, I pulled my baseball cap down and made my way straight to the VIP travellers' lounge, where I was to meet my escort to the Palace. Unlike my fellow passengers in first-class, I was scruffily dressed in faded jeans and cotton shirt. On my back was the battered rucksack that had seen me through many festivals with my actor friends. I had no idea how my escort would recognise me. I looked nothing like a princess, and very much like the person I was: a struggling actress trying to make a living.

I pushed open the door to the lounge

and glanced round at the occupants. The handful of passengers in the room looked up as I entered and quickly dismissed me as someone of no interest. Almost as one, they returned their attention to their tablets and smart-phones. I'd expected my escort to be just like one of these men, dressed in a dark suit, clean-shaven, and with close-cropped hair. Instead, a slim guy wearing biker leathers rose from his seat in the corner and came towards me. A pair of dark eyes met mine, in a grave, rather intense face.

'Elizabeth Smith?' His voice was low, so as not to be overheard in the quiet of the room, and that prickle of unease rose inside me again.

I'm used to observing people; it's something I've learned to do as an actress. Now I took in the stranger's features, tanned a deep brown, the straight shoulders and the attentive manner as he bent towards me. Despite his rather solemn gaze, there was something direct about him, and a frankness I found instantly attractive. I'd been sent alone to a

3

foreign country, where all was not what it seemed. I decided then, rightly or wrongly, that here at least was someone I could trust. I held out my hand with a smile.

'My friends call me Lizzie,' I told him, keeping my voice equally low.

He took my hand in his.

'I'm Léon. I'll be your bodyguard.'

Another jolt of nerves. A bodyguard? This wasn't something I'd expected. The director of my drama school had insisted that although what I was about to do was risky, at least I would be in no physical danger.

Léon took in my startled expression and, taking my arm gently, began to guide me out of the lounge.

'We'll talk at the Palace,' he said. 'Let's not dawdle here.' And then, as we approached the station exit, he asked, 'Have you ever ridden pillion on a motorbike?'

I flashed him another bewildered glance. It seemed a strange way to arrive at the Palace. Then I gave a mental shrug. Considering the circumstances, it was as odd as everything else.

4

'Well, yes,' I told him. 'I have my own motorbike, back in Edinburgh.'

He glanced down at me. Did I detect surprise? I remembered how reactionary the people of Montverrier were. This small Mediterranean principality was hundreds of years old, and, cut off as it was from the outside world, had yet to arrive in the twenty-first century. Despite lip service to the contrary, women here were still regarded as second-class citizens. As we approached Montverrier, I'd been the only female passenger on the train without a male escort. I'd heard it was unusual for women in Montverrier even to drive their own cars.

'You must wonder why I'm collecting you by bike,' Léon said, echoing my earlier thoughts. 'We need to keep your arrival at the Palace low key. And a biker's helmet is perfect. No one will be able to see your face.'

The glare of the sun hit me as soon as we stepped out of the station. My jitters subsided again, and I stood stock still, entranced by the blue of the sea, the sight of the palm fronds gently waving on the wide promenade, and the smartly-dressed men and women walking to and fro. I would have remained there gawping if Léon hadn't calmly but firmly steered me in the direction of his bike. I noticed as we walked that he was careful to keep our backs to any passers-by, and so, despite my curiosity, I dropped my head and kept my eyes on the ground, so that my face was further hidden. In addition, I adopted a slouching walk far removed from the Princess's upright posture. Anyone at the station that morning would be most unlikely to connect the arrival of a rather scruffy tourist from Scotland with the official appearance of Her Royal Highness later in the summer.

Léon's eyes gleamed as he handed me a helmet, and he gave a brief nod of approval.

'Very good,' he said. 'I'm beginning to see why they chose you.'

Then he was astride his powerful bike, with the engine running. It was a much larger machine than I was used to, and with my rucksack weighing me down I was forced to put my hand on Léon's shoulder to steady myself as I mounted behind him. His back was hard and steady as a rock. As I seated myself, he turned his head, brows raised in enquiry.

'OK?'

I was very far from OK. I was alone, slightly terrified, and in the hands of someone I'd only just met, but I ignored the butterflies doing their warning dance in my stomach. I lifted my thumb, and next minute we were roaring out of the station and along the coast road.

2

I took hold of Léon's waist and, with no other option, gave myself up to the exhilarating freedom of the journey. Our road wound to the left, hugging the coastline, and the breeze caused by our speed tugged at my shirt, cooling my skin. As the tarmac disappeared in a blinding blur beneath my feet, I thought how incredible it was to be here, now, riding pillion behind a bodyguard, so far from my quiet flat in Edinburgh.

Back home, it was the start of the summer holidays. The weather when I left Scotland had hardly been seasonal.

On the last day of the school term, I'd returned to my flat soaked through with a cold, misty drizzle that had been falling for days. It was in a gloomy mood that I pushed open the front door. I should have been celebrating the end of a successful year, but instead I'd just been informed that, due to cutbacks, funding for my travelling drama school was to be drastically reduced. If I couldn't find another source of investment, I faced having to cancel my appointments in September and disappointing all the schools that were expecting our return. Not only that, I would have to tell the actors who worked for me that they were out of a job.

There was a pile of letters on the doormat. I swept them up and put them on the table in the hall, intending to ignore the bills until I could face them, but one of the envelopes dropped to the floor. A hand-written address on stiff white paper read: *Ms Elizabeth Smith.*

I left the other letters where they were and slid the envelope open. Inside was the extraordinary note that would lead me to Montverrier.

Dear Elizabeth,
I have been asked to find an actor to take on a role in southern Europe this summer, and I believe you would be perfect for the part. As the contract

is for the summer months only, this should not disturb your work at your drama school too much should you accept. The role is well-remunerated, with board and first-class accommodation included.

I look forward to seeing you in my office on Monday at nine to discuss.
Yours,
Charles Ross

I turned the letter over in my hands. I hadn't heard from the director of my old drama college since I'd left five years before. Although it was a long time since we'd met, he'd been an inspirational teacher, and I'd never forgotten him. True to form, Mr Ross never forgot a pupil, either, and he'd evidently been taking an interest in my career since I'd left college.

The rain continued to pour down outside my window as I pondered Mr Ross's sudden communication. The invitation was sketchy in the details. Still, a summons from Mr Ross wasn't one you could ignore. Besides, the thought of paid work and first class accommodation in sunny southern Europe was tremendously appealing. I made up my mind to be in the director's office on Monday, bright and early. After all, what had I got to lose?

And so a couple of days later I found myself in the same corridor where I'd once waited anxiously to perform my first ever audition as a student. I felt the same sense of nervous anticipation as I knocked on Mr Ross's door.

'Ah, come in, Elizabeth,' he said, as though I'd only been gone a couple of weeks, rather than years. He indicated the chair in front of his mahogany desk, and I took a seat.

'I daresay you're wondering what all this is about.' He fixed his intelligent gaze on me. 'What I'm about to tell you is top secret. It involves an extremely important family in Europe, and it's imperative that nothing of this is ever leaked to the press. You may not discuss it with your friends or even your close family. No one, do you understand?'

I widened my eyes. I'd been expecting

some sort of role in a European film — some minor part that required my brand of Celtic looks. Nothing as mysterious as this. Perhaps this was the time when I should have got up to leave, but Mr Ross has a penetrating way of looking at you that's hard to resist. Like the fool that I am, I merely nodded.

He placed a sheet of paper in front of me and took the lid off his fountain pen.

'This is a legal document binding you to secrecy. Whether or not you take up the role offered, you must never reveal anything I'm about to tell you. I want you to read the document carefully, and only sign if you feel comfortable.'

Well, I didn't feel particularly comfortable. I don't like secrecy, and I was beginning to feel ill at ease. I stared at the paperwork for a moment or two in silence, thinking things over. I trusted Mr Ross's judgment. He would never involve a pupil in anything underhand. Besides, to be honest, my curiosity was piqued despite my doubts. I read the paper over, signed it, and passed it back to him.

'Good.'

The director reached back into his desk, this time drawing out a manila envelope, from which he withdrew a large glossy photograph. He placed the photo in front of me without speaking. The tanned, beautiful young woman in the picture was instantly recognisable. Princess Charlotte of Montverrier. The country itself is tiny, but its glamorous royal family is known throughout the world.

I looked up, my curiosity deepening.

'You recognise Princess Charlotte, of course.' Mr Ross pressed the tips of his fingers together. 'Let me fill you in on some details about Montverrier. It's one of the oldest principalities in Europe, and one of the most conservative. Women only gained the vote in the 1950s. Even today, there are no women in government, and there has never been a female sovereign. Princess Charlotte is an only child, as you know, and her mother died ten years ago. With no brothers, when King Albert dies, the Princess will become the first woman ever to reign over Montverrier. For the past three weeks King Albert has been seriously ill in hospital with pneumonia. He could die at any moment.'

I knew all this. There had been several articles in the press discussing the King's ill health and how most of the population embraced Princess Charlotte as future monarch. There were still some diehard conservatives, though, who thought it a crime against morality for a woman to be sovereign, and that the next in line to the throne should be a male cousin.

I waited for Mr Ross to continue.

'The Investiture ceremony for the next-in-line traditionally takes place on the heir's twenty-fifth birthday,' he said. 'Given the level of discontent from some quarters about a female heir, it's vital that the Investiture goes ahead this summer as planned. If the Princess is not able to take part, it will only fan the flames of those militants who say that women aren't fit to reign. Everything has been meticulously organised.'

Mr Ross was always one for a dramatic

pause, and he stopped then, his sharp gaze on mine. I was transfixed. What did a small European principality have to do with me?

'So what's the problem?' I said. 'The Princess is well, isn't she?'

'Two weeks ago, Princess Charlotte vanished.'

For a couple of seconds there was deadly quiet in the room. Now I realised why I'd been asked to sign myself to secrecy. If information about the Princess's disappearance got out — especially with the level of hostility towards a female leader from certain fundamentalists in Montverrier — it would make news around the world.

The disquiet I'd been feeling prickled and grew stronger.

'Where's she gone?' I asked. 'Has she been kidnapped?'

Mr Ross shook his head. 'Let me reassure you the Palace doesn't believe it's anything sinister. The Princess is highly-strung, and they maintain she has merely run away somewhere where she can escape the pressures. There are whole teams searching for her, but so far without success. In the meantime, the date of the Investiture draws ever nearer, and the ceremony must go ahead.' Another dramatic pause, whilst he bent his searching grey eyes on mine. 'With or without the Princess.'

I stared at him. Surely he couldn't be suggesting what I thought he might be suggesting?

'I don't understand,' I said, although I was beginning to work out where this incredible conversation was going. 'How can they expect to hold the ceremony without the Princess? She has to be there, surely?'

'Ah.' Mr Ross eyed me again with his penetrating gaze. 'Well, Elizabeth, this is where you come in.'

Another dramatic pause, while he waited for me to draw my own conclusion.

My mouth dropped open, and I was filled with the same feeling of anticipation and high anxiety I normally experience before the start of a theatrical performance.

'Are you seriously asking me to impersonate the Princess of Montverrier for her ceremony?'

'Of course I'm serious. Why should I not be? I'll let you into a secret, Elizabeth. It wouldn't be the first time I've arranged such a deception. A President taking a military salute, a First Minister at a state funeral, a minor Royal at a wedding. You'd be surprised how often such a stand-in is necessary.'

I gave a wild laugh. 'You mean you have a pool of look-alikes for state appearances?'

'Not look-alikes.' Mr Ross wrinkled his nose in disdain. 'I work with actors.'

The director was deadly earnest. He was examining me as though he were the puppet-master in some sort of travelling show. And I was the puppet.

I picked up the photo of Princess Charlotte and pointed to her gleaming white smile. 'This is ridiculous. I don't look anything like the Princess. Look at her. She's blonde, tanned and groomed.

I'm red-headed, pale, and — and perfectly nondescript.'

The director nodded. 'You have that useful thing for an actor, which is an unremarkable face.'

'Thanks,' I said. My voice was heavy with irony, but he appeared not to notice.

'And your figure is perfect,' he went on. 'We have artists who'll make you look so like the Princess, no one will know the difference.'

'But a stand-in! Surely the risks are too great?'

Mr Ross steepled his fingers. 'As far as risk goes, most of the ceremony will be perfectly straightforward. The journey to the Cathedral is in a closed carriage, and there are no cameras allowed during the Investiture. Your words will be relayed by speakers to the crowds, of course, but I know from your time here as a student you'll have no problem copying the Princess's voice. After the ceremony you'll be driven back to the Palace in an open carriage. That short ride is the only part of the occasion that may present us with

18

some difficulties, as you'll be exposed to the full public gaze.' He waved his hand dismissively. 'The ride in an open carriage is where the greatest danger lies,' he repeated. 'But we're used to smoke and mirrors in our trade. We can take care of it.'

Smoke and mirrors? The eyes of the whole world would be on me. I had confidence in my acting abilities, but it would take a pretty big cloud of smoke to stop someone with a zoom camera from guessing I wasn't the Princess of Montverrier. I opened my mouth, about to say I'd never heard such a ridiculous idea, when the director tapped an envelope on the desk in front of him.

'The Royal family understand the dangers involved,' he said, 'and they'll pay you well for your trouble.'

I dropped my eyes to the crisp envelope with its discreet Royal crest. Mr Ross slid it towards me and I pulled out the contract inside. My jaw dropped. Of course there was a risk involved, but even so, the sum offered was enormous, and out of all proportion to the task. I stared at the figures and thought of my travelling drama classes, and the enthusiasm of the kids in all the schools I visited, and how now I'd be able to keep my educational theatre going without worrying about where the next funding was coming from.

And finally I thought, really, how hard could it be to wear a crown for a day? I raised my eyes to the director's.

'OK, I'll do it.'

3

And so now, a whirlwind week later, here I was, far from the dark, gloomy alleyways of Edinburgh, rushing past the Mediterranean under a glorious blue sky towards my temporary life as a princess. I tightened my hands on Léon's waist as he picked up speed. Still keeping close to the coast, we began to climb the hill leading to the Palace. The road twisted and turned, and I bent my body with Léon's as we rounded each curve, sometimes leaning precariously towards the ground as it rushed past.

I was fascinated by the sea — such a bright blue, and so different from the grey, misty coast I was used to — and so it was a surprise when I glanced round Léon's shoulder to see we were approaching the Cathedral. Of course. This is where the Investiture ceremony would take place in a few weeks' time. My nerves began another shivering dance as we neared. It was a magnificent building, all pearly white bricks and ornate, rococo design. Not for the first time I began to doubt whether I could go through with the charade. I wondered if there was any way I could change my mind. For an instant, I would have given anything to be back in my cosy flat in Edinburgh, with the rain pattering on the window, a cup of tea beside me and a book in my hand.

But there was no halting Léon. We zoomed past, and then another sight caused my jaw to drop and my nerves to redouble. Beyond the great courtyard in front of the Cathedral someone had erected an enormous placard where everyone on the road to the Palace would see it. There, in big red letters, were daubed the words:

A KING for a KINGdom. Tradition not ABOMINATION. Say NO to a Queen for Montverrier.

There was a rough painting of a crown with an angry cross through it. Léon must have sensed the tremor that ran through me and my hands tightening around him because he slowed, throwing a glance over his shoulder. His eyes met mine briefly, but then the road claimed his attention and soon we were speeding away again.

All my pleasure in my arrival in this hot, colourful country vanished as the Cathedral disappeared behind us. Mr Ross had insisted that my stay here would involve no danger, but whoever had erected that sign was impassioned and furious. I couldn't believe a simple placard would be an end to the protest, and I began to wonder what had actually happened to the Princess. Had she really just run away? Or was she being held captive by angry protesters until after the Ceremony? I pressed myself closer to Léon's reassuringly solid frame, but my heart was pounding in my ears.

We were now on the wide avenue leading to the Palace, with rows of tall poplars reaching up on either side of us. At the far end of the avenue was the ornate ironwork fencing that surrounded the Palace gardens. Beyond, I could make out the vivid colours of an exotic flower display and a peacock strutting his way along the fence, for all the world like a miniature guard. On either side of the main gates, two soldiers dressed in white stood to attention. On their heads were white helmets plumed with gold, with the black of their guns the only jarring note.

Instead of approaching the main gates, Léon drove on, down past the side of the Palace gardens until we came to a smaller side gate, similarly guarded by soldiers. Léon halted beside them and reached into his leather jacket to pull out a battered document. The soldiers examined the paper and looked at me, their faces unsmiling. My heart hadn't stopped pounding since we passed the Cathedral. It took all my drama training to keep my face neutral and my hands steady on Léon's waist, but then the soldiers were saluting and clicking their heels, and the gates to the Palace were opening.

Léon revved the engine, and we were inside the grounds of the Palace of Montverrier. I heard the gates shut behind me with a clang, like the doors to a prison.

4

The Palace building was constructed from cream bricks and looked for all the world like a toy fort. I looked up to see the dark blue and gold stripes of the Montverrier flag hanging from one of its turrets, lifeless in the hot, still air. Mr Ross had only been able to give me a hurried briefing in the few days I'd had available, and up to now I'd seen just a handful of photos of the Palace. It was smaller than I'd expected, and more welcoming somehow, with its warm stones and flowers at the windows. My heart began to slow a little at the sight of it.

Léon brought the bike to a halt in a small forecourt to one side of the building. He dismounted first and reached out a hand to help me down. My legs were trembling, but I kept my fingers steady in his, reaching up my other hand to take off my helmet. He stopped me with a hand on my arm.

'Wait,' he said. 'We must go inside before you remove your helmet. There are too many windows looking down on the grounds.'

I looked up. He was right. There were literally hundreds of windows. Who knew what was behind them?

Léon pressed my arm. 'Don't be afraid. All will be well as long as you do exactly as I say.'

Far from reassuring me, his words reminded me that I was completely in his hands. It was an uncomfortable sensation for someone so used to independence, and I was reminded again how alone I was, and how far from the safety of home. When I didn't answer, he continued ruefully, 'I'm afraid from now on you will have to learn to trust me.'

He, too, was still wearing his helmet. All I could see were those dark eyes, which now seemed to reveal some kindness. I nodded.

'Very good,' he said. He took my arm. 'Our housekeeper, Daria, is waiting to show you to your rooms.'

We entered a side-door to the Palace. Instead of the light, spacious interior I expected, I was surprised to find myself in a dark and rather shabby corridor. My footsteps echoed on the cream and grey tiles, but there was no time to look around, because a woman dressed from head to toe in black came hurrying down a flight of stairs to greet us.

Léon ushered me forward. 'Lizzie, this is Daria.'

The housekeeper stretched out a pale hand. She had the whitest skin I'd ever seen, smooth and flawless, almost like a doll's. She gripped my fingers once, claw-like, and released them. Her eyes, almost black in her pale face, swept over me, and I was filled with another sensation of foreboding.

I gave her a warm smile I was far from feeling.

'Pleased to meet you, Daria.'

Daria nodded once, brusquely, and turned to speak to Léon in a language I didn't understand. Montverrier is a country of two languages. The official language is French, and, as my mother was French, it's a language I speak well. On the streets, though, the citizens of Montverrier speak their own dialect; a unique vocabulary found only in this tiny pocket between the mountains and the Mediterranean.

I could grasp nothing of Daria's guttural comment. To be honest, I thought excluding me from the conversation was a little rude. So, evidently, did Léon. He answered Daria in French, and I gathered we were to avoid the main entrance by taking the servants' stairs to the Princess's suite, which was to be mine for the next five weeks.

Daria led the way, with Léon bringing up the rear. He'd relieved me of my rucksack and slung it over his own strong shoulder, something I was to be glad of, as there were three steep flights of stairs to climb before we reached the door to the Princess's suite. Daria pushed it open, and I stifled a gasp of delight. Unlike the servants' stairs, the room we entered was light and airy, with three tall windows opening out onto a balcony. I wanted to see more closely the beautiful gardens Léon had hurried past, and the avenue of poplars, and so straightaway I made a beeline for the view.

Léon had stopped to speak to the housekeeper. Now he said sharply, 'Stay away from the window, Lizzie.' I halted, taken aback, and gave him an astonished look. 'Don't put yourself anywhere where someone might catch a glimpse of you,' he said. 'Not even when the make-up artists have done their work, and you begin to look like the Princess. We can't take any risks at all before the ceremony. You must get used to keeping yourself as much out of the way as possible.'

I turned to give a longing look through the window. All I could see from this part of the room was the blue sky meeting the tops of the poplars. Was this to be the whole of my contact with the outside world for the next five weeks? A bird flew past, a dark speck on the blue, and the sight of its freedom brought home to me everything I would be giving up. But I straightened my shoulders. I was being paid to do a job, and I intended to perform it to the best of my ability. And, unlike the Princess, at least I could return to normal life at the end of it.

Daria stepped into the room, her heels rapping on the parquet floor.

'Léon is right, Miss Smith. From now until the ceremony you must remain in these rooms. No one will be allowed to enter unless escorted by Léon or myself.'

Of course it made sense to keep myself apart from the rest of the Palace. The risk of discovery was too great. Still, I couldn't prevent a feeling of dismay at being cooped up in this suite for weeks, whilst the sun beat down so gloriously outside my window.

The housekeeper went on, 'The staff have been told that Princess Charlotte is keeping to her suite until the Investiture. They believe she is suffering from a nervous disorder, and that doctors have prescribed complete rest. It's vital that no one here discovers you are not the real

31

Princess.'

'And what if Princess Charlotte returns before the ceremony?' I asked.

Daria gave a small, tight shrug. 'If Her Royal Highness returns, all well and good. You will go home, and Princess Charlotte will take part in the ceremony herself.'

What a strange reply! The Princess's return would be *"all well and good."* It seemed an indifferent comment from someone who should surely be desperate for the Princess's safety. My eyes were on Daria's, but she merely gazed back at me coldly.

'And the King?' I asked.

'The King is far too unwell to leave his room in the hospital.' The chill in Daria's expression dropped another degree. 'We must pray that the King does not die before the Princess has been crowned next-in-line. If he does, it will leave the throne empty and —'

She broke off. Finally, she had shown some emotion. What was it she was afraid of? I remembered the angry words daubed outside the Cathedral. Just how dangerous were the protesters? My eyes flew to Léon, standing in the doorway. Beside the forbidding housekeeper, his presence was solid and reassuring.

His eyes met mine. 'You have nothing to fear, Lizzie.'

* * *

The tension left my shoulders. There was something uncomplicated about Léon that drew my trust. And after all, what could happen to me in a Palace so well guarded?

'Very well,' I said. 'And now I'd like to ask you both a favour. Please don't think of me as Lizzie Smith. I'd like you to start addressing me as you would the Princess.' I smiled, indicating my travel-stained jeans and flat pumps. 'It might seem strange to you, when I'm dressed like this, but I need to immerse myself in my role.'

Léon nodded and gave a small bow of his head. 'Very well, Your Highness.' I was taken aback by the promptness of his response, and so I almost missed the remarkable change in Daria's features. Her eyes flashed fury. I thought for a split second I must have imagined it. What could possibly have caused such anger?

Even after her expression returned to its blank chill, her cheeks remained mottled with red.

After a short pause, she said, 'Very good.' And then, after another telling hesitation, 'Your Highness.'

I tried to hide my dismay. I had no wish to provoke a quarrel. Over the housekeeper's shoulder, Léon continued to look at me, straight-faced. And then one corner of his mouth lifted in a brief smile and, unbelievably, he gave me a reassuring wink.

It was such an unexpected response, I almost choked on a laugh. I turned it adroitly into a cough, putting my fingers over my lips.

'You must be thirsty after your journey,' Daria said. 'I will bring you a tray of coffee and biscuits. Would there be anything else?' Another pause, before she added through thin lips, 'Your Highness?'

I shook my head. 'No, thank you, Daria. Some coffee would be lovely.'

Léon opened the door, and the housekeeper's heels tapped away down the corridor. My bodyguard waited, head on one side, until the sound of footsteps had completely disappeared. Then he said quietly, 'You mustn't mind Daria. She's devoted to Princess Charlotte. She will find it hard to see someone else in her place.'

I chewed my lip. This was an unexpected complication. I hoped Daria wouldn't make my time here even more difficult than it already was.

Léon remained in the doorway, hands by his sides, his helmet tucked under one arm. Several seconds ticked past, and I wondered what on earth he was waiting for. Finally he broke into the glimmer of a smile. 'I'm sure you want to rest and freshen up, Your Highness. But I can't leave the room until you give me permission to do so.'

'Of course,' I said. 'You may go.' I tried

to answer in the way the real Princess would have done, but the words were awkward, and I felt my cheeks go pink. It was all very well asking Léon to think of me as the Princess, but I still had no idea how to act like one. 'Oh, dear,' I said, falling back into my natural manner. 'I have a lot to learn, don't I?'

The look on Léon's face told me all I needed to know. There were barely five weeks until the ceremony. Five weeks had seemed like a long time to be away from home, but now it seemed not nearly enough to learn everything.

After Léon had gone, I gazed around the room that was to be both my home and prison for the next five weeks. It was elegantly furnished, but there wasn't much sign of the Princess's personal presence. The furnishings were a mixture of the antique — a silk-covered chaise-longue and a walnut cabinet — and the bland — a few official photos of the royal family, and a couple of land-scapes of Montverrier on the walls. Not much to go on for a guess at Princess

Charlotte's personality, or for a clue to her whereabouts.

I thought again of the angry placard we'd passed on the journey to the Palace. I hoped wherever the Princess was, that she was in no danger. And, more than anything, I hoped she would return safe and well in time for the ceremony.

5

After finishing my coffee I showered and changed into a pale blue summer dress I pulled out of my rucksack. There was an enormous wardrobe in the Princess's suite. I'd opened it briefly and discovered row upon row of dresses carefully stored in plastic wrappers. One wall was devoted to shoes and handbags, all of exquisite quality. In the bedroom there was a smaller wardrobe filled with other less formal wear; capri pants and flowing cotton skirts, t-shirts and silk scarves.

After unpacking the meagre belongings in my rucksack and hanging them next to the Princess's collection of finery, I wondered what to do next. There was a bookcase in the sitting-room, filled with the latest best-sellers, and a rack full of magazines, but I was too on edge to concentrate on reading. I was just wondering if it would be all right to move a little

closer to the window and look outside
— I could peek out from behind the cur-
tain, surely? — when a knock at the door
almost made me jump out of my skin.

I opened it to find Léon. He'd changed
out of the biker leathers and was wearing
dark trousers and a white t-shirt. I'd
thought him slender when we first met,
and that his torso was bulked out by
his leathers, but even without his thick
biker jacket his chest was broad and
hard. A tattoo was just visible beneath
the sleeve of his t-shirt. I was so struck by
the change in him it was an instant before
I realised there were two other people
standing behind him.

'These are your hairdressers, Your
Highness.'

I pulled the door wide to let in two
rather serious-looking, fresh-faced
young men, very different from my stub-
ble-chinned, chatty hairdresser at home.
They entered in silence, without greeting
me, and I showed them to the Princess's
enormous bathroom. As they set up their
tools, I returned to the sitting-room to

find Léon had taken a seat on one of the silk-covered sofas and was waiting, arms crossed over his broad chest.

Mindful of what he'd told me earlier, about having to wait for the Princess to give him permission to leave, I said, 'There's no need for you to stay, Léon. You may go, if you wish.'

He looked at me, in that steady way he had that I was coming to recognise.

'As long as there are other people in your suite, I stay with you. And you must never, ever allow anyone into these rooms unless I'm present. Do you understand?'

I understood only too well the importance of remaining hidden. Even so, I felt an irrational desire to protest, to tell Léon he was making me feel like I was a prisoner, and he the gaoler. Still, I couldn't afford to let myself descend into claustrophobia. There were still weeks until the ceremony. I turned on my heels to join the waiting hairdressers.

After leaving drama college I'd played a few lead roles in the theatre, as well as one or two parts on television. I'd been sprayed green and given warts for the Wicked Witch of the West, worn a bump as a pregnant teenager, and even had my head shaved for a role as cancer patient in a hospital soap. All these were nothing, though, to the transformation I was about to undergo.

The wall-length mirrors in the Princess's bathroom reflected my pale complexion. I met the hairdressers' critical eyes in the glass as they examined my wavy red hair. The Princess's hairstyle, at least, was relatively easy to copy. The process took a couple of hours, but when the hairdresser brushed off the last few remaining strands of red hair from my neck and I finally stood up from my chair, I had a chic honey-blonde bob. I stared at my reflection, turning my head this way and that. My normal hairstyle was tousled and a little unruly. I no longer looked like me. I still didn't look like the Princess, either, but it was a start.

When I returned to the sitting-room, Léon rose to his feet. At first I wondered if the hairdresser had made a big mistake.

He took one look at me and a flicker of dismay crossed his face. I patted the back of my head, where the line of the bob lay neat and crisp. I felt just as though I'd returned from my own hairdresser's, and was ridiculously anxious for Léon's opinion, which was silly. I was here to do a job, and so I bit back the words, *'Don't you like it?'* that were hovering on my lips.

But perhaps I'd imagined Léon's initial reaction. He gave a brief nod and said merely, 'Very good.'

My unruly curls had gone, but my make-over was far from finished. Throughout the rest of the day, Léon would leave and return with yet another silent make-up artist. I was manicured and pedicured; my brows were plucked, arched and dyed black; I was moisturised and depilated, and my teeth whitened until they pinged when I opened my mouth. Every operation on my body was carried out with seriousness and attention to detail, and a complete lack of regard to my own presence in the room. I began to feel like a mannequin, devoid of personality. It didn't help that the make-up artists were completely silent.

Whenever I'd been made up in the theatre in the past, by the time my nails had dried I'd have found out all about the make-up artist's in-laws, her latest holiday to Greece, and which actors are sleeping with whom. In turn, I'd have given her the gossip on all my other acting jobs and my plans for decorating my flat.

By contrast, the make-up artists Léon brought into the Princess's suite were quiet as the grave. If I asked a question, they merely answered yes or no. They showed no curiosity about the fact I was being made over to look like the Princess of Montverrier; they simply applied their skills to my body in a swift, efficient manner that was completely chilling.

As one of the artists examined a recent photo of the Princess, I began to wonder where these people had come from. Then I remembered what my old director had told me about his network of stand-ins. Were all these people in Mr Ross's pay?

If so, perhaps in the past they might also have worked on actors I knew; acquaintances of mine from college. I imagined a group of stand-ins across Europe, all ignorant of each other's roles, with Mr Ross holding all the threads together like a puppet-master. I itched to ask the make-up artists who else they'd made over, but their forbidding manner discouraged me from speaking at all.

Finally, after turning me this way and that way for hours, the artists packed all their equipment away and left. I stood alone and naked in front of the mirror after they'd gone, examining the woman I'd now become. I glowed all over with a deep brown tan that had been carefully applied with a spray. My eyebrows were two fine arcs, and my lips had been plumped into a rosy bow. When I smiled, my teeth gleamed. I no longer recognised the person in front of me.

I'd made much study of the Princess while I was still in Edinburgh, watching several video clips. She had a slender, ethereal grace, and it seemed to me that despite my physical transformation, my reflection was a little too solid and down-to-earth. There was still a lot of work to be done before I could pass for her.

As a test, and to see if I might eventually step inside the Princess's skin, I tried one of her mannerisms; that sudden, charming smile she had for the reporters, which failed to light her eyes, and which would vanish as quickly as it had come. I smiled — and yes, there she was! I tried it again, entranced by my reflection. The likeness was completely uncanny.

I heard Léon return from escorting the last of the make-up artists to the Palace gate. By now I knew his firm knock on the door. I threw on the white robe they'd left me and made my way through the sitting-room to let him in.

When I opened the door his dark eyes widened for a moment in astonishment at my transformation. I almost laughed at his reaction, like a little girl at a fancy-dress party, but then the reality of it all hit me with force. I was no longer Lizzie Smith. I was beginning to lose my true self. I should have felt excited at the thought of stepping into a new role, but instead, I remembered the angry placard on the road past the Cathedral, and my precarious position, and I shivered, wrapping my gown more tightly around me.

★ ★ ★

It was late by the time the make-up artists had finished their work, and I was beginning to feel hungry. I was about to ask Léon what I was to do for meals, when my question was answered by a knock on the door. Daria entered with a selection of dishes and cutlery on a silver trolley, bringing with her the most delicious smell of roast meat and herbs.

Like Léon, the housekeeper's eyes widened when she saw how I'd been transformed, but her expression quickly became cold and even a little disdainful. Perhaps she thought it was disgraceful of me to imagine I could ever replace Princess Charlotte, no matter how well

I tried to disguise myself. It was a relief when Daria placed the trolley next to the table in the sitting-room and left without speaking.

I lifted one of the domed lids to find everything was duplicated: two plates, two sets of cutlery, two meals, two desserts.

I frowned, looking up at Léon. 'What's all this?'

He shrugged. 'My orders are to remain with you.'

'What, all the time?'

This time a short nod.

'Even at night?'

For once, he looked a little discomfited. I glanced around. My suite had only one bedroom.

'I will sleep here.' He indicated one of the sofas.

I was beginning to understand that my bodyguard was a man of few words. There was a second or two's silence as I stood there, foolishly clutching the silver lid. But I didn't feel the need for my improvised shield. On the contrary, I found the thought that Léon would be

47

sleeping outside my room each night, like some knight in a medieval castle, immensely reassuring.

The tantalising smell of food wafted from the tureens, and I remembered how long it was since I'd eaten. Léon, too, must be hungry. I guessed he must be waiting for me, in my role of Princess, to invite him to eat. For a gaoler, he was a patient man.

'Shall we have dinner?'

He gave a small bow of the head. 'Your Highness.'

6

From then on, Léon was always by my side.

At first the intimacy was strange and awkward. We had to share the bathroom, for example. Although Léon was punctilious about removing all trace of himself, there was still a lingering aroma of mint toothpaste and an indefinable maleness about the place when I entered it.

And then there was the fact that he was sleeping in the next room. When I climbed into bed that first night and sank down on the pillows, my body was exhausted, but my mind was racing as though I were still on the back of Léon's motorbike. The unfamiliar bedroom was unsettling, and the sight of my bare, tanned arms on the covers gave me a sense of being inside the wrong body. But funnily enough, it was the thought of Léon's calm, solid presence within reach that finally helped me sleep.

My first morning in the Palace, I awoke to bright sunshine streaming through the window. I sat up with a start. My automatic reaction was to reach for my mobile phone to check the time, but my phone was back in Edinburgh, where I'd left it in the care of Mr Ross. As part of the terms of my contract, I was to have no outside contact with the rest of the world. My story was that I was on a walking holiday in the Alps, and out of reach. Depressingly, there were few people who would miss me. Mr Ross knew both my parents had died some years previously. I have an aunt and several cousins, but when I informed them of my holiday, they showed little interest. My few close friends in Edinburgh had their own plans for the summer and merely wished me *bonnes vacances.*

I got out of bed and put on my dressing-gown, feeling more alone than I had done the day before, but when I entered the sitting-room and saw Léon's familiar figure at the table, a large pot of coffee beside him, my spirits rose. He was beginning to feel like an old friend. I beamed a smile at him.

Léon pushed back his chair and rose to his feet. 'Good morning, Your Highness. Did you sleep well?'

'Not really, Léon.' I ran a hand through my hair. The neat bob was dishevelled and sticking up in soft tufts. 'It's the strangeness of everything.'

He took in the shadows under my eyes. 'It will be a difficult few weeks. Do you think you will manage to remain cooped up in this room until the ceremony?'

I told him I would, although I didn't feel at all confident. My actor's training must have worked, though, because Léon nodded approvingly.

'There's a lot to be done,' he said. 'But first, breakfast. Daria has brought us a tray.'

He came round the table and pulled out a chair for me. After my initial shock at being immersed so completely in Léon's company, I was beginning to find him a restful person to be with. He didn't speak much, but he had a way of second-guessing what I wanted. He offered me items from the breakfast tray before I even opened my mouth to ask. I wondered if it was his bodyguard's training that made him so observant, and was curious to find out more about him.

'How long have you worked as the Princess's bodyguard, Léon?'

'I don't work for the Princess, Your Highness.' He split open a croissant and began to spread it generously with butter. 'Besides, I would be ashamed to let one of my charges disappear without a trace.' He frowned. 'I don't know what her own bodyguards were thinking. I hope they've been sacked from their jobs.'

I had to smile at the vehemence of his reply. 'So where did you work before, then? You're from Montverrier, aren't you?'

He nodded. 'My mother is Italian, but my father is from Montverrier and I grew up here. I did my national service here, also.' He glanced up at me with a wry smile. 'Although we don't exactly have a big army. National service in Montverrier mainly consists of standing outside the Palace in full uniform trying not to faint in the heat. After the army, I did some training in Switzerland. That was an eye-opener.'

Léon took a large bite of his croissant. I waited for him to continue, but it appeared his breakfast had claimed his attention.

'An eye-opener?' I prompted. 'Did you work in Switzerland?'

He nodded, and began to tell me about the enormously wealthy family whose children he had guarded.

'To be honest, I wasn't so much a bodyguard as a nanny. The parents were often away, and I would play football and video games with them.' He smiled. 'Even read them stories at bedtime.'

I laughed. 'How sweet. I can imagine you reading Little Red Riding Hood, Léon. You must be relieved to know bedtime stories aren't part of your duties here.'

His eyes met mine over the breakfast things and he held my gaze for just an instant too long. I had the ridiculous image of Léon reading to me, lying beside me in my large bed in the next room, and I felt my skin begin to warm.

There was a rattle at the door, and the housekeeper pushed it wide. Her black eyes flew to me, dressed in my robe as I was, and then flicked to Léon, like a lizard's. I could tell she was angry. Unnerved, I straightened up. Léon continued to drink his coffee, unmoved.

'There is work to be done this morning, Your Highness.'

Apart from Daria's thin-lipped use of my title, I'd given up hope of her ever showing me the deference due to royalty. Still, it would be nice not to feel intimidated every time she entered the room.

I narrowed my eyes. 'I'm well aware of the programme, thank you, Daria. I have been through everything necessary with Mr Ross in Scotland. And now if you wouldn't mind removing our breakfast things.' I rose from the table, glancing enquiringly at Léon. 'That is, if Léon has quite finished?'

Léon stood with me, leaving his half-empty coffee cup on the table. He nodded. We watched Daria clear our trays away in silence. After the housekeeper had left the room, I continued to gaze after her, my back ramrod straight.

'That was well done, Your Highness.' Léon's quiet words brought me back from the dark direction my thoughts were taking me. 'You are beginning to act like a princess. I'm glad that you refuse to let Daria intimidate you. Sometimes I swear she acts as though she were one of the Royal family herself.'

Léon's words gave me pause for thought. Perhaps I'm a little foolish. You probably think I'm stupid, even. But with all the rush to leave for Montverrier, I had never questioned who had actually sent the request to Mr Ross for a stand-in for the Princess. At the time, I'd assumed it must be the King. Now I realised he was far too ill. It couldn't have been the Princess herself, as she was missing. So who was it who had set the wheels in motion?

'Léon,' I said. 'How did you come here? I mean, who asked you to be my bodyguard?'

'I received a letter from Daria at my home in Switzerland.'

'Daria.' I knitted my brows. I suppose it was believable that Daria, being so close to the Princess, should be the one to arrange security for her stand-in. But who had approached Mr Ross? Was that also Daria? Why would a Palace housekeeper be the one to make such a request? Who was really in charge in the Palace, in the absence of the King and Princess?

Léon must have sensed my bewilderment.

'Let others concern themselves with Royal politics,' he said calmly. 'We have our own work to do.'

I tried to dismiss my concern as easily as Léon, but there were too many uncertainties. I'd hoped matters would become clearer the longer I stayed in the Palace, but the truth only retreated deeper into the mist.

7

Léon was right, though. I was being paid to do my job, and there was still much to be done before the ceremony.

Although superficially I now looked like Princess Charlotte, I was still a long way from "being inside her skin," as I liked to think of it. Mr Ross and I had discussed how best to immerse myself in my role, and together we had come up with a schedule.

For the first few days, every morning, after Daria had cleared away our breakfast tray, Léon would set up a screen in the sitting-room. Mr Ross had provided me with me with several memory sticks containing video clips, and I would load them into a laptop and sit and watch the Princess move about on the large screen, hour after hour.

Here she is descending the steps of a plane in the Caribbean, in fashionable, wide-legged trousers and sunglasses. The expression on her face is hard to see beneath the broad brim of her hat. She stands at the top of the steps and gives a wave to the crowds; an elegant lift of the hand, palm outwards, fingers very slightly spread. I practised this same wave in front of the mirror until it came as naturally as breathing.

Another clip showed the Princess at the film festival in Cannes, walking away from the cameras, down a long red carpet. I studied every movement of this walk; the way her feet turn very slightly outwards, like those of a dancer; the way she holds her head, turning it lightly to take in her surroundings; the way she glances over her shoulder with a small smile.

And so on and so on, through many, many more: Princess Charlotte tripping up the steps to the Cathedral for Sunday Mass; chatting with friends in the stands at a race track; dancing at a charity ball; greeting the Queen and Prince Philip in a state room in the Palace. On and on the videos played, and I repeated her movements over and over again. And all the while, as I metamorphosed myself into someone I was not, Léon sat on the sofa, his arms crossed over his broad chest. Occasionally he would move to stand by the window to check the scene outside, and I would ask him what he could see, but it was always the same answer: sun, sky, poplars.

Once I asked Léon if he weren't tired of watching the Princess leaving and arriving at various glamorous locations time and time again. He surprised me by answering, 'I've been learning, too. Play the next clip, and I'll show you.'

As the next video began to play, Léon pointed out all the other people in the crowd that I hadn't noticed myself, engrossed as I was in the Princess's actions.

'See, here are her bodyguards.' He indicated a couple of well-built men with serious faces, one walking in front of the Princess as she made her way along the promenade in Nice, and one just behind her.

I gave Léon a sideways look. 'They're muscular and they're wearing shades,' I said. 'That doesn't mean they're body-guards. They could be anyone.'

'No, look again.' He pointed at the screen. 'Those two men are the only people not watching the Princess. They're watching the crowds. And if you look carefully you'll see a bulge beneath their jackets. They are carrying guns. I've seen these same two guys on a lot of the clips you've played.'

He waited for the video to play out and the next to start. 'See, here they are again. And watch how the one in front — the darker guy — moves those two people back in the crowd. He does it well, without causing confrontation. They're doing a good job.'

Léon stood, arms folded, a frown on his brow. A silence fell as I pondered his words. If the Princess's bodyguards were doing such a good job, then how was it she had disappeared? It didn't make sense. It seemed to me that outside the walls of my suite the Palace was a web of the unknown. As if on cue, right there in the next clip was Daria, all in black, clipping along like a beetle behind the Princess's graceful figure.

I paused the video and turned to face Léon.

'Léon, what do you think is going on here in the Palace?' I asked him. 'I mean, the real truth?'

He dropped his hands to his sides and looked at me. 'My job is to protect you on the day of the ceremony. No harm will come to you whilst I am your bodyguard. Trust me.'

There was a dark, serious light in Léon's eyes as he spoke. I nodded slowly. I did trust him. I did believe he would try his utmost to keep me from harm. It was only later that night, as I lay awake watching a few wisps of cloud drift past the moon through my window, that I realised Léon hadn't really answered my question. What did he know about what was going on in the rest of the Palace? It was true he was there to protect me on the day of the ceremony. But it was also true that he made sure I never left my suite, and that I spoke to no one unless he or Daria authorised it.

The clouds sailed past outside my window, leaving a glorious night sky behind them, black as jade, and sprinkled with a thousand stars. It was a sky such as I never saw in my northern city, and despite its splendour, as I gazed on it, I was overwhelmed with longing for home.

8

It's strange how quickly a person can become accustomed to new surroundings.

Within a few days of my arrival, I had fallen into a routine every bit as regular as my motorbike ride to work each day through the streets of Edinburgh. It helped that Léon was as punctual and as reliable as the soldiers outside the Palace, who paraded in the grounds every day at twelve o'clock on the dot, the sergeant's commands penetrating even the thick plate windows to my suite.

One morning, a week or so after I arrived, I entered the sitting-room to find Léon engrossed in a book. I must have expressed surprise, as up until then I'd never seen him reading.

He rose from the breakfast table as I entered, his expression a little bashful.

'I don't normally read when I'm working. Books are too much of a distraction.

I become involved in a story, and I lose concentration.' He glanced around the suite. 'But here, I know you are safe in your bedroom during the night. No one can get to you except through this room. I can relax.'

'Oh, Léon,' I said, feeling guilty. 'And now I'm awake, and I've spoiled all your pleasure in your book.'

He shook his head, drawing out a chair for me. 'It's no matter. My book will always be there.'

'What are you reading?'

He hesitated. 'It's a Roman military history.'

I was touched to find he was a little embarrassed. Perhaps he thought I might mock his interest, but I was curious to know what he found so fascinating.

'Really? Have you always been interested in that time in history?'

And so Léon began to tell me how he'd stood inside the ruins of the Coliseum in Rome with his Italian mother as a teenager, and how he'd wondered about the might of an Empire that could build such a magnificent building two thousand years ago and send armies across the world. He'd started devouring anything to do with Roman history, and especially to do with their military. He was fascinated by their efficiency and organisation.

'Do you know they conquered most of the countries around the Mediterranean, but they never conquered Montverrier?'

I poured myself a coffee, shaking my head. 'Why not, I wonder? Surely the tiny army of Montverrier couldn't withstand the might of Rome?'

'No. It wasn't military might that kept out the Romans. It was a trick.'

I looked up, my attention caught. 'A trick? What sort of trick?'

'The only way the Romans could invade Montverrier was by sea, since the mountains provide too difficult an obstacle. But even a fleet of Roman ships travels slowly. The fishermen of Montverrier knew in advance that the soldiers were approaching. There was time for the people to prepare. The Romans landed, expecting at least some resistance, and found a country of walking dead.'

I spluttered and swallowed my coffee. 'What a fantastical tale,' I said. 'Do you mean zombies?'

He smiled. 'Yes. In a way. The country's elders met the Romans on the beach and told them to go back. They said that all their crops and drinking water had been cursed, and the spirits sucked out of the citizens by malevolent gods. Of course the Romans suspected a trick. They sent a party into the King of Montverrier's palace. Once there, they met with no resistance. Everywhere the soldiers went, the citizens shuffled past them, dressed in rags, their skin blue, their eyes vacant. It must have been a chilling sight, but it didn't stop the Roman army. They helped themselves to whatever they wanted: women, gold, wine, food. Until finally they, too, became walking corpses.'

I opened my eyes wide. 'Now you're kidding me. Did this really happen?'

He chuckled at my reaction.

'Yes, really. The citizens had tricked them. The wine the soldiers stole was poisoned. There is a root that grows in the mountains that has a powerful effect on the mind. If you eat it, you lose consciousness of your own surroundings, and yet your body remains active. Of course, the people of Montverrier knew better than to eat the drug themselves. It can be fatal. They simply put on an act.'

Here Léon stood and walked a few paces towards me, his eyes white and rolling, his arms limp by his sides. It was such a convincing performance, I drew back involuntarily in my chair.

'Stop it, Léon!'

He laughed and sat down again to continue his story.

'Once the poison began to take effect, the elders herded the soldiers back to the waiting fleet. They stumbled along, blind to everything around them. The elders told the rest of the Roman army, "Look! Your soldiers have fallen foul of the gods, as we warned you they would. You must leave, now, before your own souls are sucked from your bodies." It must have been a terrifying sight, all those years ago. Hundreds of men, eyes vacant, not knowing their comrades. The Romans who'd remained on board ship gathered them all in and fled back to Rome, as fast as they could.'

'What an amazing story! And you're such a good story-teller, Léon. It's no wonder your Swiss charges wanted you to read to them. Your zombie gave me chills down my spine. You should be an actor.'

It made me smile to see Léon blush with pleasure. 'Thank you, Your Highness,' he said gravely. The twinkle in his eye undermined his serious tone, and I laughed out loud.

'If the people here are so full of tricks, I see I must be on my guard in Montverrier,' I said. Then I sobered quickly, and glanced up at Léon. 'That's an amazing story, about the Romans. That all the people of a country could act together in such a cool fashion, and pull the wool over the eyes of an entire invading army. I can't believe the men of Montverrier just stood back when the soldiers came and let them take what they want, including the women. It seems a little bit chilling.'

Léon put his head on one side, considering. 'That's true,' he said slowly. 'But it's a small country, and the people have always had to rely on cunning rather than strength.' Then he glanced at me teasingly, changing the subject. 'And in any case, what about Scotland? The Romans never invaded your country, either. In fact, they were so frightened of you, they had to build a big wall to keep you out.'

I laughed at this, and when Léon asked me to describe my home, I began to wax lyrical about the Castle and King Arthur's Seat, and the views to the sea, and the road up the coast to the Highlands. I painted such a homesick picture of Edinburgh, and Léon was so fascinated by all I had to tell him, that it came as a shock when Daria entered to take away our breakfast things. We broke apart almost guiltily.

Daria's black, beady eyes darted between us, and I felt my cheeks go crimson, as though she'd caught Léon and me in a passionate embrace, which was ridiculous. We'd only been talking. I rose to my feet and kept my voice as cool as I could.

'Good morning, Daria. Thank you for the breakfast.'

★ ★ ★

Léon stood when I did. Unlike me, he seemed completely unflustered by Daria's entrance. He moved away to the window.

Daria began stacking the breakfast things. 'What news of the Princess?' I asked her.

Her eyes darted towards me and away. 'Nothing. Our people are still searching. You have a speech expert coming this morning. Mr Ross has arranged it. What time shall I send him to you?' Then she added as an afterthought, 'Your Highness.'

I knew perfectly well that a speech master would be visiting that morning. It was all part of the schedule I'd discussed with Mr Ross. It was on the tip of my tongue to say so to Daria, but then I gave a mental shrug. The housekeeper seemed determined to cling to her passive aggressive manner, and confrontation wouldn't help us in the few weeks remaining.

'Send him up in half an hour,' I said coolly. 'Thank you, Daria.'

* * *

I turned to go to my room to get dressed. Léon was leaning back against the wall, his expression blank, but as I passed he gave me an approving nod.

9

After watching hour after hour of video clips, I had mastered the Princess's movements and mannerisms well enough to pass scrutiny on the drive to and from the Cathedral. I knew exactly how to hold my head erect, how to lean forwards as I offered the crowds a smile and a wave, how to mount the Cathedral stairs with a light step, my back straight and my chin just lifted. Even the Princess's own father would need to look closely in order to tell the difference between us.

There was now just the little matter of the ceremony itself. The Archbishop of Montverrier would do most of the speaking during the service. The Princess had only a few lines to say, before and immediately after the Archbishop placed the crown on her head, but her every word would be relayed to the crowds outside and scrutinised across the world.

Mr Ross had organised a speech expert to ensure that when the Princess's voice crackled over the speakers outside the Cathedral, no trace of plain Lizzie Smith from Edinburgh would be heard.

Dr Graham was brought to my door by Daria. He was a man of around sixty, with a full head of grey, fluffy hair and eyes like an owl's behind steel glasses. Ironically, for a man who was an expert in speech, he barely said a word in conversation during his time with me. Another one of Mr Ross's team of silent staff, I guessed.

Dr Graham brought with him a disk containing samples from the few occasions where Princess Charlotte's voice had been recorded. Before attempting the Princess's voice for myself, I sat in silence, listening over and over again as the professor played back her clear vowels and precise consonants. As an actress, I'm used to projecting feeling in my speech. After listening to the Princess time and again, one thing struck me forcibly. Her voice contained no emotion at all. On first hearing the disk, I put this down to nerves. Perhaps Princess Charlotte was shy of speaking, and had merely learned her speeches off by heart, forgetting that she was addressing real people. But the more I listened, the more I began to wonder. When a speaker is nervous, there will be a tell-tale tremor in the voice, a hesitation, or sometimes a stifled giggle. The Princess's voice was completely steady, and completely cold.

"I'm delighted to be here at the Royal Children's Society..."

"As patron of the Montverrier Ballet, I was deeply moved by your performance..."

And, most chilling of all, *"It is with great sadness that we remember today the Queen, my mother..."*

I began to wonder what this young woman could be like, whose voice was so empty of emotion, even when she spoke of the death of her own mother. It was one of the most difficult voices I'd ever had to mimic, and I struggled. As I repeated the words of the ceremony for Dr Graham, I couldn't help but inject

74

some feeling into them.

"I, Charlotte, Princess of Montverrier, do declare my loyalty, and life and limb I will devote unto you..."

The professor would pick me up time and time again. 'No, no, no. I hear Lizzie Smith from Edinburgh. Get rid of your own emotions and become the Princess.'

In the end, I decided the best thing to do was to recite the words as though I were relaying a shopping list over the phone. That way, I could be sure they were precise, and yet devoid of any feeling.

Mastering the Princess's speech patterns was hard work and took longer than I'd anticipated. It took several days of endless repetition of the words of the ceremony before Dr Graham was satisfied enough with my progress, days in which I became increasingly frustrated with myself, and with my situation. As I immersed myself more and more in my role, the walls of the Princess's suite closed in on me, leaving me feeling stifled and a little afraid of the cold, unfeeling creature I was becoming.

Through it all, I was glad of Léon's steadying presence. My days transforming myself into the Princess were full of intense concentration. The evenings, though, were a different matter. After Dr Graham had left for the day, and Daria had removed the remains of our dinner, Léon and I would be left alone in the Princess's suite. There was no outside entertainment for us. No wifi, and not even a television. I would have liked to have watched the news, at least, in order to find out how things were in Montverrier, and whether the protesters had taken any other action apart from putting up the placard.

In my first week at the Palace, I'd asked Daria if it would be possible to have a radio. The housekeeper had put on her most contemptuous expression.

'There is no need to concern yourself with outside events, Your Highness. You must focus on your role in the ceremony. Everything else is a distraction.'

My sudden plunge into isolation had

badly affected my spirits. I lost my temper a little.

'Says who?' I asked. 'Who has the right to decide all this, and tell me how I can and can't approach my job?'

She raised her brows. 'I have my instructions, Your Highness.'

'Who from?' I insisted.

There was the merest hesitation. Daria dropped her gaze from mine and resumed her task of clearing the plates from the table. 'Mr Ross believes it's better for you to have no outside influences.'

'Mr Ross?' I stared at Daria. This was the first I'd heard of it. When we drew up our schedule together, Mr Ross had mentioned nothing to me about having to cut myself off from all news of the outside world.

I glanced over at Léon, but he merely shrugged, as though he knew no more than I did. I opened my mouth to protest, and then thought better of it. Perhaps they were right. Perhaps if I saw reports of bad feeling against the Princess, it would disturb my concentration, and make me even more anxious about the ceremony.

In any case, there was nothing I could do to move Daria, and so in the evenings, Léon and I were left in silence. For the first week or so, I leafed through the Princess's collection of novels and tried to read, but my mind was coiled and alert. I was unable to concentrate, and found myself reading and re-reading the same pages.

When I finally put my book down one evening and heaved a sigh, Léon glanced up from his Roman history.

'What is it, Your Highness?'

'I just don't know what to do with myself, Léon. I can't sit still to read. My mind is jumping like a flea in a circus.'

He rose from the table and went to the long walnut cabinet against one wall, where he proceeded to open one of its doors. To my surprise, he pulled out a chess board and a mahogany box of pieces.

'Chess?' I cried in dismay. 'If I can't even read a book, I'll never be able to concentrate long enough for a whole game of chess.'

'Nonsense.' Léon set the board on a small side table and began calmly setting out the pieces. 'Chess is wonderful for focusing the mind.'

And so, reluctantly, I took up a place opposite him and begun studying the board. It was a long time since I'd played. My father had taught me when I was just a child, but I hadn't played since he died. My father's old, battered set was nothing like as ornate as the Princess's. I picked up each marble piece one by one and examined it curiously. All the figures were foxes, and each one was a work of art. The king was ferocious and snarling, and his queen a cunning vixen. Even the pawns were intimidating cubs, brandishing swords. I found the whole set a little disquieting, like everything else in Montverrier.

Still, I pushed forward one of the pawns, and we began to play. It didn't take long for me to realise that Léon was a worthy opponent. He applied the same cool concentration to the game as he did to his job as bodyguard. I found myself studying his face, instead of the game; the way he rested his chin on one fist; the small frown that puckered his brow, and the long, dark lashes that hooded his eyes as he gazed at the board. His physique was strong and spoke of action, but his movements were surprisingly contained. There was even something graceful in the way he leaned forward to lift a piece in his long fingers. I became so engrossed in watching Léon, that first evening we played, that I lost the game within a very few moves.

The next evening was different. Léon had been lulled into a false sense of security by my lapse in concentration. I was playing white, and he blocked all my advances with a routine set of play that was easy to predict. When I left a path open to my queen, he took it with his rook in a swift move, glancing up at me as though disappointed in my lack of skill.

I pretended to be cast down at my failure to protect my vital piece. I studied the board, my chin resting on both my hands.

'Oh, dear,' I said. 'How stupid of me to expose my queen like that.' I frowned and pushed forward a knight, into the path of Léon's king. 'But just a minute,' I asked, feigning innocence. 'Isn't that .... checkmate?'

I lifted my head, blinking.

Léon stared at the board in astonishment. Then he laughed out loud. 'You little devil!'

It was the first time I'd seen Léon laugh. His eyes met mine, alight with amusement. His serious mouth spread wide in a smile that transformed him, showing gleaming white teeth and deepening the laughter lines running down his cheeks. All the stiffness left him, and his chest rumbled with mirth.

My eyes were drawn to his mouth and the curve of his lips. I don't know how long I stared at him; it could have been just an instant, or whole minutes. Time seemed to stand still. All of a sudden I realised he was no longer smiling.

'It's getting late, Your Highness,' he said quietly. A faint flush crept over his cheeks.

He dropped his eyes at last and began picking up the heavy chess pieces and replacing them in their box. 'Tomorrow will be another long day.'

I stood then. 'Good night, Léon.'

'Good night, Your Highness.'

Léon didn't stand, as he usually did whenever I left the room. He didn't look up, either, but kept his eyes on his task, placing the pieces carefully one by one in their velvet box.

After I'd got ready for bed and was lying awake, shifting restlessly, that night, more than any other, I was conscious of Léon's presence in the suite. I heard him go into the bathroom, and then a little while later, I heard his footsteps retreat to the sitting-room. I pictured him lying on his uncomfortable sofa and wondered what thoughts went through his head in the darkness, before he fell asleep. Was he lying alert, ready to prevent anyone entering the room? By this time, we'd been thrown together a long time. I realised how little I knew of him.

I realised, too, that after all this was over I'd miss Léon's quiet, gentle presence very much.

10

Five weeks is a very long time to be cooped up in one suite of rooms, no matter how luxurious the furnishings.

Léon must have been more resilient than I. Nothing seemed to trouble him. He was able to remain perfectly calm and still for hours at a stretch. Every day when I woke he greeted me in the same easy manner, and yet I, on the other hand, became increasingly restless as the weeks wore on, to the point some days of wanting to run to the door, wrest it open and race down the corridor, screaming my way to freedom.

The lack of physical exercise was also a strain on my mental state. I walked up and down the long sitting-room every day, practising my role as the Princess, but this was a slow stroll, on light footsteps, and I missed the vigorous workout to be gained from a brisk stride up

Arthur's Seat back home in Edinburgh. In the mornings, before breakfast, I practised yoga in my bedroom in order to keep my limbs supple. Caught up in my own isolation as I was, selfishly I hadn't stopped to consider how even more restricting these four walls must be for a man like Léon.

One morning I woke much earlier than usual, in the throes of a terrible nightmare. I'd dreamt I was walking up the steps of the Cathedral, with the hot sun blazing down on my head. The crowds were silent, radiating malevolence. As I turned to give them the Princess's wave, they began to jeer and boo. And then, in that way there is in dreams sometimes, there was the real Princess, dressed in jeans and a shirt, standing on the steps in front of me. She lifted her head, and the look in her eyes was one of such ice-cold rage I woke in horror, my heart beating like a drum.

I rolled out of bed without thinking, hoping Léon's down-to earth presence would banish the fear brought on by my over-active imagination, but I'd forgotten how early it still was. I pushed open the door to the sitting-room and found Léon stretched out on the polished floor, dressed only in his shorts. His hands were behind his head, and he was lifting himself off the ground in a set of rapid pushups. His eyes were half-closed in concentration, and he hadn't noticed me enter. I stood for a moment, my hand on the door frame. Léon's legs were tanned and muscular, and his thighs bulged and lifted with each lift of his torso. My eyes were drawn to his tight stomach, rippling with strain, and then to the beads of moisture on his chest that mingled with the sprinkling of hairs.

I wrenched my gaze away, beating a swift, silent retreat to my bedroom. Then I lay on my bed, gazing up at the ceiling, the pounding in my heart sounding in my ears. It was a long time before the image of Léon's physical exertion left my head. Even when I closed my eyes, the sight was imprinted on my retina. The tattoo on his arm — the one that was usually only just

visible beneath the sleeve of his t-shirt
— was of a stylised bird in flight. I saw it
rising and falling, the wings beating with
the flexing of his muscles.

Eventually I stretched into a few yoga
poses to calm myself, and my caged
thoughts settled. All that day, though, I
remained on edge. My dream, and the
four walls around me, oppressed me beyond all endurance.

When Léon pulled out the chess board
for our game later that night, I leapt to
my feet.

'Léon, how can you stand it?' I cried.
'I don't think I can bear another moment
cooped up in here. I need to feel some
sun on my skin. Breathe in some fresh air.
Get out of this stifling room. *Anything*!'

Léon just stood there, his face grave as
usual. He made me feel as though I were
a child having a tantrum, and in fact I
would have liked nothing better than to
run at him and beat his chest until he felt
the same agony I did. I breathed in and
out slowly, but the walls of the suite were
crowding in on me, and I lifted my hands

to my head, almost moaning aloud.

'Is it really so bad?' Léon came towards me and pulled down my hands, holding them in his own.

I nodded miserably. His strong fingers pressed mine, and he leaned closer. For a breath-taking moment, I thought he was about to hold me in his arms, but then he stepped back, my hands still in his, and looked at me, a twinkle in his eye.

'Well, there's no sunshine,' he said, lifting his head in the direction of the window, where the curtains were drawn against the night. 'But how about some fresh air?'

I brightened, my lips parting in anticipation. 'Really? How?'

'We could take a couple of cushions and sit outside on the balcony. Just this once.'

It's a measure of how desperate I was to escape the Princess's suite that even this small freedom made me draw in my breath in a gasp.

'But you must be quiet as a mouse,' Léon warned.

I pulled my hand out of his to put a finger to my lips.

'You won't hear a sound, I promise.'

I ran to my room to fetch a cardigan to throw over my shoulders. I realised I had never been out after dark in Montverrier. I'd arrived in blazing sunshine. What would the temperature outside be like at night? Hot and sultry? A fresh breeze from the sea? Perhaps it sounds ridiculous, but I was coiled up with excitement at this small step outdoors.

By the time I returned, Léon had thrown open the balcony doors and switched off all the lights in the sitting-room, so that we wouldn't be seen. I stumbled as I entered, my eyes not used to the dark, and started when he caught my arm.

'Ssh,' he said, his voice a whisper against my cheek.

He led me towards the door onto the balcony and made me crouch down as we stepped over the sill. I stifled a giggle. It felt as though we were escaping a school dormitory. Léon had set a few cushions against the stone balustrade. He guided me down, so that I was sitting out of sight, with my back against the cool stone. I had no need of my cardigan. The evening air was warm and still.

He bent to whisper in my ear. 'Look up.'

I tilted my head. A full moon hung above the roof of the Palace, bathing us in a cool glow. All around, twinkling and dancing, were layer upon layer of stars, stretching away into infinity. It was as though we were suspended alone above the city, with nothing to prevent us float-ing up and plunging our hands right into the middle of the Milky Way. I breathed in the warm air from the sea and felt drunk with exhilaration.

I turned to Léon, and saw my own shining eyes reflected in his. 'Thank you,' I breathed.

Léon's eyes darkened, shimmering wide and midnight black. The moon bathed his face, highlighting the planes and angles, and leaving his mouth a firm, carved line. He leaned towards me, reaching out a hand to settle my cardigan more securely around my shoulders. His fingers brushed my neck, and I shivered.

'You're not used to the evening air,' he said, his voice a murmur. 'Perhaps we should go back inside. Daria would never forgive me if you caught a chill.'

'No,' I said in a firm whisper. 'If I go back inside that room again, it will kill me. Please, Léon.'

He nodded. 'Very well. Just a little while longer.'

And so we sat there in silence, the two of us, and this escape into the night, sitting side by side with Léon, listening to the faint heartbeat of the city and the murmur of the sea — this brief escape was one of the happiest moments of my entire life.

I brought my knees up and rested my hands on top of them, leaning back against the stone wall of the balcony. I don't know how long we sat there. Neither of us felt the need to speak. Occasionally Léon shifted position, stretching his legs out in front of him. I heard his steady breathing, and the flap of a bird's wings overhead, and time seemed to stand still. Perhaps I even began to drift into sleep. I had the impression we were riding in the basket of a balloon in the night sky, far above the world, away from all tension and stress. For the first time since I'd arrived in Montverrier, my mind was completely relaxed.

And then a new noise drifted upwards from the city. A staccato splutter, repeated three or four times. Léon shot bolt upright.

'Oh, fireworks,' I said. 'How lovely. Such a shame we can't stand and watch …'

He hauled me to my feet in a flash, pressing his hand on my back so that I remained crouching. 'Get inside.'

There was the distant whir of an engine approaching. Léon bundled me over the sill of the balcony and pushed me into the sitting-room, closing the thick plate door after him. Then he dragged me by the hand and forced me down on one of the sofas, with its back to the windows. I could see nothing except the silk cushions.

'Stay there.' His eyes were wide and fixed on the sky outside.

The engine's rumble grew louder, and I recognised the clatter of a helicopter's blades. My heart began to race, thumping in hard, tiny beats against my rib-cage.

'What's happening?' I kept my voice to a whisper, even though the doors were shut. Léon didn't answer, and so I tried to sit, to lift my head over the back of the sofa, but he pressed down again on my shoulders.

'Stay where you are,' he said.

As he spoke, the roar of the helicopter grew nearer, and then the room was filled with a harsh white light. The noise of the whirling blades grew so loud, it seemed the helicopter must be hovering right outside our window, over the very place where we'd been sitting. I gripped the cushions. Léon's hand continued to squeeze my shoulder, steady and reassuring.

And then, as quickly as it had come, the helicopter vanished, the sound of its engine drifting away over the sea. The sitting-room was plunged into darkness again, and the only sound was my own rapid breathing and my pulse thrumming in my ears. Léon released his grip on my shoulder and stood, his eyes still fixed on the window.

'What was that?' I asked. My voice was breathless with fear.

'Nothing to worry about. A police helicopter.'

'But why?' My mind raced back to the noise I'd thought was fireworks. 'Was there shooting in the city?'

He met my gaze, obviously not wanting to cause me anxiety, but I caught hold of his arm.

'Léon! Tell me.'

He nodded reluctantly. 'Those were gunshots we heard. Not fireworks.' He released his arm gently from my fingers. 'I must speak with the Palace security.'

I thought he meant to leave the room, and had to bite my tongue to stop myself from begging him not to leave me alone, but instead he made his way to the cupboard in one corner of the sitting-room where he kept his own belongings. He drew out a slim, hand-held device, and was about to speak into it, when there was a short rap on the door that almost made me leap out of my goose-fleshed skin.

Before Léon could get to it, the door opened, and Daria stood in the doorway. Although it was late at night, she looked neat as ever in her black suit. Her face was white as marble in the dark of the room, and her black eyes flicked from Léon and back to me, before flying to the window, where the moonlight flooded in, pooling in great silver rectangles on the polished wooden floor. We had left the curtains drawn back in our haste to get inside.

Without saying a word, she marched over to close them. With her hand on the cord pull, she stopped stock still for a moment. Her attention was caught by the cushions, lying scattered on the balcony floor where we'd left them. She breathed in, with a sound like a hiss, and pulled the curtains shut. Without the moon's light to illuminate it, the shadowy room was plunged into darkness, but the house-keeper appeared to have the instincts of a bat. A couple of seconds later, she switched on the lamp on the desk, and her white face appeared out of the gloom.

Again her eyes darted from Léon to me.

'You will have heard the helicopter, Your Highness,' she said. 'There is no need for alarm. A routine search of the city before the ceremony.'

'We heard gunfire,' I said.

'There were no guns. Some yachts have arrived in the harbour. The people have begun celebrating with fireworks. I'm sorry if they disturbed you.'

I looked at Léon quickly. He was stand-ing immobile, his arms crossed over his chest. I couldn't tell what he was think-ing, or whether he believed Daria or not.

'What about the protesters?' I insisted. 'I know there are people in Montverrier who are against the Princess. Is there fighting in the city? Has she been found? Does anyone have any idea where she is?'

Daria's face was as cold and eerie as the moon had been.

'There is no need for you to concern yourself. Your job is to take part in the ceremony, where you will be well guarded.' She turned her attention to Léon. 'And your job is to make sure Miss Smith sees no one until she leaves the Palace. No one, do you understand? Even stepping onto the balcony is too great a risk.'

I caught the reddening in Léon's cheeks, even in the dim light cast by the lamp. It was a reprimand, but he took it calmly, merely bowing his head once.

Daria turned to me. 'There are only a few more days until the ceremony. You must get some rest.' Then she added tightly, as though against the grain, 'You have worked hard, Your Highness.'

She made her way to the door. I waited for a few seconds after she'd closed it, then I looked at Léon.

'Do you believe her? Were they really only fireworks?'

'Perhaps.' He shrugged off the question and moved so that he was standing close to me, his expression serious. 'You did very well this evening, Your Highness. You showed no fear, and you did as I said. As long as I am your bodyguard, whatever happens during the ceremony, no harm will come to you. Do you trust me?'

A lump rose in my throat. It wasn't the first time Léon had asked me this question. I was afraid, but I nodded.

'I trust you.'

Our eyes held for a few moments. I didn't know it then, but it was a statement I would come to regret bitterly.

11

I had been willing these five weeks away, but now, as the day of the ceremony approached, perversely I wanted time to linger.

My nerves were jittery. It didn't help that Mr Ross's team of silent make-up artists came back to prepare me, reapplying the tan which had begun to fade during my confinement, freshening up my manicure and retouching the roots of my blonde bob. Their lack of conversation unnerved me.

A couple of days before the Investiture, the housekeeper brought someone new with her — a designer to fit my dress. I'd been most anxious about practising walking in ceremonial robes, and had had visions of having to support a long, heavy ermine cloak and an enormous crown, like the one worn by Princess Elizabeth during her coronation. Daria had informed me that I had no need to worry about managing stiff robes; that my dress would be quite simple.

I was surprised to find that the designer, a small, fussing man who spoke as little as everyone else I'd been in contact with, brought with him just a cloth carrying case and a small bag. We retired to my bedroom for the fitting. I stepped into the gown — a long, flowing, simple dress in fine white silk, cinched tightly at the bodice and fastened with tiny buttons in the shape of rose-buds.

The designer clapped his hands together in appreciation of his own handiwork, walking round me several times, tugging here and adjusting there.

'A little tuck here,' he muttered to himself, inserting a couple of tiny pins in the fabric either side of my waist.

He drew a pair of matching silk slippers out of the bag and placed them on my feet. And then, last of all, the crown, which I wouldn't wear until the Archbishop placed it on my head during the ceremony.

I held my head quite still as the designer fitted it into position. The crown was surprisingly light; more like a tiara than the cumbersome affair I'd expected. It was fashioned out of gold strands, spun together in the form of flowers, with diamonds at their centre. One large diamond glittered in the midst of them all. I moved my head gingerly from side to side. The crown stayed in place. Now to test it properly. I opened my bedroom door and, with the designer fussing and clucking behind me, began a slow procession into the sitting-room.

Léon was on the sofa in his usual patient pose, arms folded across his chest. When I entered, he rose to his feet, dropping his hands to his sides.

'Your Highness.'

The expression on his face was remote; nothing like the Léon who had sat on the balcony in the dark, gazing up at the night sky. He bowed his head.

I made my way down the sitting-room, my crowned head erect, my skirts swishing over the wooden floorboards.

All trace of Lizzie Smith had vanished. For the first time, I had managed to get inside the skin of Princess Charlotte of Montverrier.

★ ★ ★

The evening before the ceremony, I found myself entirely alone in the suite. Léon had been entering and leaving for much of the day. There was much to organise with the Palace security before the ceremony, he told me, and he wanted to ensure all was in place for the short ride to the Cathedral. In order to do so, he needed to travel the route several times himself. I would have loved to have been able to step outside with him, and to discover for myself the mood of the city. Just to have felt the fresh air on my skin again would have been wonderful.

But Daria had made all that impossible, of course. And so when Léon left me alone once more after our evening meal, I did the next best thing to going outside. I waited a few minutes until I was sure his footsteps had disappeared down the stairs, and then, against all his instructions, I switched off all the lights and tiptoed over to the window.

It was a marvellous sight. I could almost feel the atmosphere of anticipation in the city. The poplars on the avenue were illuminated in the gathering dusk with soft lighting, and beneath them an excited crowd of onlookers were already staking claim to the best places for the procession. Sleeping bags were spread out on the warm flags, candles flickered, and the sounds of music and laughter filtered up through the glass doors. To the west of the Palace, and just visible on the horizon, was the harbour, where wealthier guests had arrived in their yachts. The lights from the decks sent cheerful reflections bobbing and dipping in the waves. A few fireworks crackled and raced upwards, adding sparks of red and gold to the stars clustered in the sky.

I pressed my hand to the glass. It was a relief, after the terrible evening when the helicopter had swept over the Palace, to see that the festivities appeared so good-natured. And regarding my transformation, I knew in my heart I had done all I could, and that, from afar, not even the Princess's closest friends would guess at the deception. Yet despite this, I was filled with the most crippling fear, far worse than any stage-fright I'd ever yet experienced. I dropped my hand from the window, shivering with cold. What if something went wrong?

A step sounded behind me. 'I warned you to stay away from the window, Your Highness.'

I leapt round with a guilty start. I'd been so enveloped in my fears, I'd failed to hear Léon enter. One look at his face showed me just how upset he was at my disobeying his instructions.

'But they're so far away, Léon ... '

He reached across without speaking and drew the heavy curtains closed. His unusual brusqueness caused me a twinge of shame at causing him concern. I covered it by blurting out the first thing that came to mind.

'Isn't it strange, Léon? All those people will be sleeping soundly on the pavement tonight, and I'll be up here in my soft bed, wide awake, worrying about everything that could go wrong.'

He switched on the lamp at the desk, then returned to tug at the drapes, making sure no chink of light could get through.

'Uneasy lies the head that wears a crown,' he quoted absently, his hands busy with his task.

'Henry IV.' I glanced across at him. After all these weeks thrown together, Léon was still full of surprises. 'I had a role in that play once when I was at drama school. My first big production. The night before I didn't sleep a wink.'

I went to the desk, and my eyes fell on the lines of the ceremony. I twisted my fingers together. 'How I wish I were back in my flat in Edinburgh right now, and with all this over.'

Léon didn't reply. Ever since I'd arrived in Montverrier, he'd been a constant presence. Silent, reliable, ever watchful, and rarely showing any emotion. Today would be our last evening together. I took in Léon's dark features, the slight hook to his nose, the grace in his movements as he straightened himself, and knew just how much I would miss my faithful shadow.

'How about you, Léon?' I asked on impulse. 'What will you do after the ceremony?'

He raised his head, regarding me for a moment or two before revealing, 'I have a house on the west coast of Italy, between the sea and the mountains. I'll ride down the coast road on my motorbike, the smell of the sea and the bougainvillea in my nostrils, looking forward to a meal of steak and red wine, and to a few weeks doing nothing but swim in the Mediterranean.'

I smiled, a broad, un-princess-like grin that almost reached my ears, and banished the fear I'd been feeling.

'That sounds perfect,' I said. 'I didn't know you had such a poetic soul.'

'A man would have a heart of stone not to feel the poetry in such a place.' He

106

hesitated a moment or two before adding softly, 'But in fact, I have nothing against being here, in this present moment.'

His dark eyes rested on mine for an instant, and then his mouth turned down, and he said, 'Time to rest. In twenty-four hours all your hard work will be done.'

He moved to leave, throwing over his shoulder, 'I have one or two things still to see to. I'll ask Daria to bring you some warm milk. It will help you sleep. Pleasant dreams, Your Highness.'

After Léon had gone I wandered restlessly round the sitting-room, picking up and replacing objects at random. Léon's Roman history was lying on a side-table where he left it, and I flicked through it absently, remembering the story of how the citizens of Montverrier fooled the entire Roman fleet. The irony wasn't lost on me that I was about to embark on a similar deception, and that the loyal subjects lapping like waves on the outskirts of the grounds had no idea that their Princess was an imposter.

I moved to stand before the gilt mirror

above the cabinet. A person I'd come to recognise as myself gazed back. I'd become used to the deep tan and the black brows shaped into elegant arches. My eyes were a little greener than Princess Charlotte's bright blue, but not so different that anyone would notice. There was still something missing, though; something I'd tried hard to replicate, but failed. My eyes glowed with too much emotion. Try as I might, I couldn't empty them of feeling, as the Princess appeared to do.

I stared at myself, wondering just what my double was doing this evening. Where was she?

A knock on the door interrupted my thoughts, and I turned, expecting Daria with the warm milk my bodyguard had promised. To my surprise, Léon himself entered, bearing a tray with a steaming mug and a plate of biscuits. He carried it over to the desk and laid it down. He seemed more than usually serious.

'Elizabeth,' he said.

It was the first time he'd said my full

name. The halting way he spoke it was strangely endearing. I moved over to where he was standing by the desk.

'What is it?'

'I know you're anxious about tomorrow. Perhaps you are concerned about your personal safety. If so, I want you to know that you have nothing to fear. You will never be in any danger whilst I'm your bodyguard.'

'Oh, Léon, of course I know that,' I exclaimed. I reached out and took his hand. 'I never had any doubt in you.'

Léon's stiffness left him, and the corners of his mouth lifted, almost in a smile.

'Good. You have nothing to fear, remember that.' Then, in a gesture completely without affectation, he lifted my hand and kissed it. 'Sleep well, Your Highness.'

The impression of Léon's warm lips on my fingers stayed with me long after I'd gone to bed. For a long while I lay awake, listening to the distant sound of the crowds mingling with music and the noise of revelry on the yachts in the harbour. My thoughts were far from the day ahead. I was thinking of Léon, and how after the ceremony he would ride down the coast road to his house in Italy, and I would never see him again.

12

The day of the ceremony dawned.

I threw on my robe and went into the sitting-room for breakfast, expecting to find Léon sitting at the table as usual, with his pot of coffee beside him. He rose as I entered, and I did a double-take. He was dressed in a dark suit and tie, the white of his shirt a crisp contrast against his tanned features. Of course, I'd forgotten that Léon, too, would have to dress for the occasion. He looked so different. More remote. Formidable, even.

He pulled out a chair for me. The usual easy atmosphere between us was gone, and my heart was wrenched with sadness at the loss of it.

I took a few sips of coffee and picked at my croissant, leaving more crumbs on my plate than actually made their way to my mouth. Léon, too, was subdued, and it was a relief when Daria appeared at the door, returning with the designer and one of the make-up artists.

The next hours were spent having my hair styled and make-up applied, and I vowed when I returned to Edinburgh I wouldn't look in another mirror again for months. I was becoming heartily sick of the sight of myself.

Finally, at ten minutes to eleven precisely, the moment I'd been preparing for — the moment an entire team of staff had worked towards — had arrived. Daria opened the door of the Princess's suite, and I stepped out into the corridor, my silk dress rustling against my heels.

With all my anxiety about the procession to the Cathedral, I'd forgotten I would have another ordeal to face before I entered the avenue of poplars: meeting the Palace staff, whose presence I'd avoided so rigorously all these weeks. To my relief, the corridor outside the Princess's suite was empty.

With my heart in my mouth, I followed Daria. She led me in a different direction to the one I'd arrived in, turning right outside the suite, away from the servants' stairs, and along endless quiet corridors. Every door we passed was closed. It was as though the whole Palace had been abandoned. The unexpected silence sent shivers down my spine.

And so we made our way in procession, without speaking a word; Daria at the front, then me, and then Léon bringing up the rear, until we reached the top of a splendid flight of stairs. Although no one at all was there to see us, I made sure to lift the hem of my dress in exactly the same manner the Princess would have done. We began to descend.

There wasn't a single sound to be heard in the whole of the Palace except for our footsteps. Down and down we went, our steps in unison, until we reached a grand, echoing hallway, tiled all in marble. Several enormous oil paintings on the walls gazed down on us. Apart from the presence of these ghostly ancestors, the hall was empty. During our entire walk from the Princess's suite, we had encountered not a single soul.

But I had no time to ponder on the missing staff, because all of a sudden the double doors were opened, letting in a flood of light, and there were two footmen, dressed in dark blue livery, waiting in the courtyard. It was eleven o'clock precisely. Daria dropped back to let me pass. The heat rose in waves from the stone flags, and a bright sun beat down on my bare head as I stepped through the doors. I blinked in the unaccustomed light, casting a brief glance at the blue sky I had only seen through glass for five long weeks. To my starved eyes, its colour was a miracle of purity.

The carriage was waiting, gleaming gold in the sun like something from a fairy tale. Two white horses, large and proud, snorted and stamped at its head. Everything had the quality of a dream, and it seemed to me as though I were outside my own body, gazing down at Princess Charlotte of Montverrier as she left for her ceremony.

And then Léon was by my side, and the cool fabric of my dress floated around my ankles as he handed me into my seat. I felt Léon's fingers press mine — the merest touch of reassurance — before he followed lightly behind me. I sank back into the carriage's blue silk seat, and the horses swept through the gates.

Léon's attention turned to the crowds as we emerged onto the avenue. A great roar went up, and in the bright Mediterranean sun everything took on a vibrancy and intensity such as I'd never before experienced. The deep green of the poplars stirring gently overhead, the vivid sky where seagulls whirled and cried, the gold and blue of the Montverrier colours, hanging from every lamp-post.

The crowds waved and called out to me from behind the barriers. I leaned forward, returning their well wishes in the manner I'd practised so long, with a smile and a graceful wave, palm forward, the fingers of my hand slightly spread. Children sat on their parents' shoulders, clutching flags, whilst others clung to the slender trunks of the poplars.

The carriage rattled down the avenue

before rounding the corner into the square between the Mediterranean and the Cathedral. What a magnificent sight lay before us! The sea was a glittering expanse of brilliant blue and silver in the sunlight, and the stones of the great Cathedral a blinding white. A red carpet had been laid down for my arrival, lined on each side by trumpeters dressed in gold and blue. A group of maids-in-waiting, all in white, were at the bottom of the Cathedral steps to greet me.

As we drew to a halt, a voice crackled in Léon's ear-piece, and he spoke into his device. And then the carriage door was open, and two footmen helped me alight. The maids-in-waiting darted forwards to arrange my dress with deft fingers while the trumpeters sounded their welcome. Another great cheer went up from the waiting crowds, and it was time to begin the long procession into the Cathedral.

I didn't dare turn my head to see what had become of Léon, but I sensed his protective presence, ever watchful, as I walked away. I reached the top of the stairs, my head erect, my shoulders straight, and passed inside alone. The interior of the Cathedral was blessedly cool. I had an impression of light, and gold, and wonderful colour, but I kept my eyes fixed ahead.

The sound of the last trumpet died away. There was a muffled shuffling and rustling from the pews, and then hundreds of guests rose to their feet. The organ swelled in the notes of the first hymn, and the choir's angelic voices rang through the Cathedral. I thought fleetingly how impossible it was to fear anything in surroundings of such magnificent beauty. The sun streamed through the stained glass windows, spilling colours of ruby, emerald and sapphire in my path. As I progressed up the aisle, the scent of roses filled the air. All my weeks of preparation had come to this, and I was filled with a sense of calm.

I took my place, seated in my throne on the altar, my hands held lightly in my lap. The Archbishop stepped forward and began the first words of the service.

13

I have no real recollection of the moment the crown was placed on my head, or of hearing the Archbishop speak the words that confirmed Princess Charlotte as next-in-line to the throne of Montverrier. I remember my answer ringing clear and true, and a muffled cheer going up from the crowd. And then there was the fear gathering again in my chest as the end of the ceremony approached, and it became time to face the most hazardous part of my deception: the drive to the Palace in the open carriage. It was an effort not to tremble as I stood and made my way down the aisle.

The congregation rose and the doors to the Cathedral were flung wide, letting in a vast beam of sunlight and a burst of trumpets. I stepped out into the heat, holding my crowned head high. Once more the crowd erupted into cheers. It was now mid-day, and the sun was at its peak. The light reflected from the sea was blinding.

Relief washed over me like a wave at the sight of Léon waiting for me by the door of the open carriage. Under a thousand watchful eyes I couldn't demonstrate how happy I was to be reunited with him, but a brief look passed between us, and Léon nodded once as I stepped past him and up into the carriage.

All my pleasure in the ceremony evaporated in the too-revealing sun. I kept my smile in place and waved to the crowds as the carriage left the square. Léon sat in the far corner, scanning the throng. The short trip along the avenue seemed endless. The poplars shivered; a thousand cameras clicked and whirred. I expected any moment that someone would stop and shout, 'Fake!'

There was a flurry of unusual movement in the crowd, and for a heart-stopping moment I thought my nightmare had come true, and someone had recognised me as plain Lizzie Smith. Then everything happened with the dreamlike quality of a slowed down film.

Léon pushed me to one side, and I found myself face down on the seat of the carriage, with Léon on top of me. At the exact same moment, there came a noise like a rocket exploding. For a split second afterwards, there was silence, and then screams from the crowd. The horses shot forward, and my head was flung back violently against the seat. I heard a long, staccato volley of gun shots.

Léon murmured in my ear, 'Stay down, Lizzie.'

Several thoughts unfurled in my mind in order, with a strange slowness, as though we had all the time in the world. I realised only later that I'd thought everything all at once, in a split second.

First, I registered that Léon had called me Lizzie. His use of my name, and the sound of his voice, filled me with an exhilaration that had nothing to do with the events around me. Then I registered the shots, and guessed that someone had tried to kill me. Or perhaps there were two separate people trying to kill me. Or a team of two. Or several people lying in wait along the route, and I would never make it back to the Palace.

My heart began to race with terror, until Léon spoke again in my ear. 'Don't be afraid.'

His hand circled my waist, and he was lying over me protectively, so close I felt the gun he wore press into my back. His breathing was steady, but as the seconds ticked by and the horses raced onwards, his heartbeat quickened a little, and the hand on my waist tightened.

Then we were passing through the archway of the Palace, and I heard the heavy doors of the courtyard swing to behind us with a clang. Léon righted himself, guiding me with him into a sitting position. He reached up to straighten the crown on my head, where it had slipped to one side, and as he did so his eyes held mine.

'Are you all right?' he asked quietly.

I nodded, but my hand shook as I pushed back the lock of hair which had fallen over my forehead. The next minute there were voices and people calling out, and a dozen pairs of hands to lift me down. Léon leapt from the carriage and disappeared into the waiting throng, speaking urgently into his device.

I dragged my eyes away from his retreating back to find myself completely alone in a crowd of people I didn't know. The Palace staff — so strangely absent when I'd left that morning — now filled the courtyard. I hadn't been this close to others since I was enclosed in the Princess's suite five weeks ago, and I stepped back, pressing myself against the carriage. The crowd fell silent. Everywhere I looked there were eyes watching me, and for a few seconds I was numb with fear.

And then the people in front of me moved aside, their feet shuffling on the stone slabs, and my fear turned to shock. I was standing face to face with a carbon copy of myself: a slim, blonde woman, whose dark, elegantly-shaped brows were raised in appraisal of me.

Princess Charlotte of Montverrier ran her bright blue eyes down my length, from the crown on my head to the silk slippers on my feet, and back up to meet my astounded gaze.

'I congratulate you, Miss Smith.'

The Princess's voice carried cool and clear in the silence, so near in tone to my own, and yet so empty of all emotion. Her eyes were bluer than my own green-tinged irises, and as chilling as the ocean depths. Behind the Princess stood Daria, black and silent as a spider.

I opened my mouth, but no words came out. It was as though I were in some sort of nightmare in which I tried desperately to speak, but no sound was forthcoming. The faces of the crowd pressed closer, waiting, and still I couldn't move. I could make nothing of what was happening. Why was the Princess here? I gazed around. Where had all these people come from? Why was no one shocked to see that the Princess had a double, and that the woman who had just stepped out of the carriage was an imposter?

And then the obvious answer filtered slowly into my dull mind. I caught Daria's eye, and I could tell she knew the exact moment the truth had dawned on me. What a stupid fool I'd been! There was a glint in her black gaze that might almost have been sympathy. The Princess's features, by contrast, held no compassion, only a remote curiosity, as though she were watching an animal in the zoo, and wondering what it might do next.

'You were never missing,' I told the Princess, my voice dulled with shock. 'You were here in the Palace all along.'

Princess Charlotte gave a nod that was more a bow of the head.

'A necessary deception, given the circumstances.'

My shock turned to anger, and I drew in a breath. Before I could speak, I heard someone call my name, and then, to my surprise, there was the director of my drama school, pushing his way through the crowds.

'My dear Elizabeth,' he said.

His usual composure had completely vanished. His hair was ruffled, and his eyes were round behind his glasses. He was even panting slightly. To my amazement he pushed past the Princess as though she didn't exist. He caught hold of my hand.

'You must believe I had no idea of this deception. If I'd had any knowledge that you would be put in danger, I would never have agreed to it. Never!'

I'd never witnessed Mr Ross lose his self-possession in any way. He gripped my hand, overwrought.

'Why?' I asked him. 'Why did they do it? Why keep me locked in a room, and not tell me the truth? I don't understand!'

'I'm so sorry, Elizabeth.' His voice was harsh and rasping. 'It was all a trick. A most base deception. The Princess arranged for you to take her place in the ceremony. She was determined nothing should get in the way of her claim to the throne.'

The truth, when it came, was brutal in its force. 'So if anything went wrong — if the protesters succeeded — I would be the one to die?'

I turned round, horrified eyes on the Princess. She met my gaze without emotion, even lifting her slim shoulders in a light, elegant shrug.

'It was important for the future of Montverrier that the protesters were brought out into the open and caught. Now I will reign as Queen.'

The blood ran to my heart.

'It was all a lie!' I gazed round at the silent staff, hundreds of them, all looking at me, all aware for weeks that their Princess was alive and well, while I was shut up in her suite, a worthless decoy. All those times I'd been told not to leave my rooms, it was because I might find out somehow that the Princess was not missing, and was living and breathing in the very same building.

And then I remembered Léon, and how he'd insisted I remain in the Princess's suite, and this was the cruellest blow of all. Bitterness at Léon's deception rose in my throat, almost choking me. I lifted my hands to my head and pulled off the crown, hurling it behind me so that it landed with a dull thud on the cushions of the carriage.

'Elizabeth!'

Mr Ross attempted to catch hold of my arm, but I escaped his grasp and pushed past the Princess and her housekeeper. A gap parted for me in the throng, and I made my way at a half-run towards the steps to the Palace.

Once inside I increased my speed, leaping, panting and gasping for breath, up the three flights of stairs to the floor where the Princess had her suite. In the unfamiliar layout, I rushed down endless corridors, throwing open doors until finally I rounded a corner and found my bearings. I entered the rooms that had been my prison for weeks, closing the door behind me with a thud.

I went immediately to my old battered rucksack and began to pile in the clothes I'd brought with me. Lies and deception! I was sick of it all. I caught sight of myself in the mirror, still in my long white dress, my cheeks flushed beneath the sprayed-on tan. My fingers tore at the rose-bud fastenings until the silk slid down my skin, tumbling in a crumpled heap on the floor. Then I pulled my old jeans out of the wardrobe. I remembered Léon telling me not to be afraid, and my heart twisted like a knife. And I had told him I trusted him! Everything was a lie, but I'd thought that Léon, at least ...

I gave a choked cry and rushed to dress myself in my jeans and my old faded vest top. With my face scrubbed clean of make-up, I began to look more like myself. Only the tan and the blonde hair-cut belonged to the Princess. I grabbed my baseball cap out of my rucksack and pulled it down low over my brow. Then I cast a swift glance around my room, making sure I'd left nothing of my own behind.

Outside the window, the sun continued to catch the waves in the harbour, spar-kling right the way to the horizon. Despite the richness of the room and the beauty of the view, I wouldn't miss anything at all from my stay in Montverrier. *Nothing at all*, I told myself. I left the room, closing the door firmly behind me.

14

The destination board at Montverrier train station indicated there was still another half an hour to wait.

I sank onto a bench, propping my rucksack beside me. It had proved surprisingly easy to leave the Palace — far easier than it had been to gain entry. The soldiers had cast a cursory glance in my direction and opened the gates. After that, I'd joined the throngs of people making their way home. All talk was of the attempt on the Princess's life. I kept my head down, and no one in the crowd gave me a second glance.

There was still a danger, though, that someone might mistake me for Princess Charlotte, and so I leaned forward on the bench, elbows propped on my knees, keeping my eyes on the ground and my baseball cap well pulled down. I tried not to count the minutes.

The station concourse was full of travellers going home after the ceremony, and there was the constant tread of feet hurrying by. I kept myself occupied by studying the hundreds of pairs of shoes that passed through my line of vision, trying to guess the personality behind each one. This sort of game would normally keep me entertained for hours, but today the loafers and the wedge heels, the hi-top trainers and the black patent leather began to blur in front of me. There was a pain in my chest that refused to budge, and I felt hot tears well and roll down my cheeks.

I squeezed my eyes shut and sat for a while like this, letting the train announcements and the hurly burly of the busy station wash over me, until I realised one of the passers-by had come to a halt beside my bench. A shadow fell over me. I opened my eyes warily to find myself gazing down at a pair of biker boots. Boots that were attached to a pair of muscular, leather-clad legs. I went perfectly still. The boots moved, and Léon sat down beside me.

I kept my gaze resolutely on the ground. For a long minute, Léon didn't speak. Then he leaned forward, resting his elbows on his knees.

'I didn't know. That the Princess was alive and well, and in the Palace, I mean. I believed all their lies.'

I glanced sideways at his profile. Léon's lips were pressed together. A pulse beat rapidly below his jaw line. I remembered the slow, strong beat of his heart as he protected me in the carriage. I looked away.

'You were so calm when the shots came. As though you were expecting someone to try and kill me.'

'Why shouldn't I be calm?' he said. 'I told you no harm would come to you. You were safe.'

I digested his words in silence. It was true, he had kept me safe by covering me. But while I was protected, Léon had taken a terrible risk in leaving his own body exposed. Had he really felt no fear? I cast another sideways glance at him under my eyelashes. Whatever his reaction under gunfire on the avenue, there was nothing calm about him now. Beneath his stillness he was filled with suppressed agitation.

'I quit my job,' he said.

I sat up straight, then.

'You quit? Why?'

'Because they lied to me, and I believed them. What sort of bodyguard fails to protect his charge like that? Instead of protecting you, all I did was lead you into danger.'

'Léon, you saved my life!'

He shrugged, without replying. His hands were twisted together, and I felt an urge to place my own hand over them. We had both been betrayed.

'Do you remember that story you told me?' I asked him. 'The one about the Roman army, and the trick the people of Montverrier played on them? I was thinking of that story as I walked down to the station. You shouldn't blame yourself, Léon. We've been outclassed by people who are used to surviving through deception and cunning.'

Léon said nothing. I don't know if

my words helped him at all. His hands remained gripped tightly together, so that the whites of his knuckles showed through.

'What will you do now?' I asked him.

He relaxed his shoulders a little.

'Go travelling for a while. Maybe look for work elsewhere.' He looked down at the ground, gazing at the marble floor as though it were the most interesting thing in the world. 'I heard Scotland's nice.'

My heart did an enormous somersault. I turned my head and stared at him, at the bands of colour on his cheeks, the pulse beating rapidly in his throat. Was it possible that Léon, my cool, collected bodyguard, was actually nervous?

He shuffled his booted feet.

'How about you?' he said, still not looking at me. 'What are your plans?'

'I'm taking a couple of weeks' holiday.'

I studied his averted profile. His jaw clenched once.

'With friends?' he asked.

'No.' He raised his head, then, and I gave him a small smile. 'I thought I might travel down the west coast of Italy. Somebody told me how beautiful it was.'

Léon stilled, a light burning in the dark eyes resting on mine.

'The smell of the sea and the bougain-villea,' I quoted softly.

The silence that fell between us stretched, full of delicious anticipation. Then Léon, too, broke into a smile — the first heartfelt smile I had seen him give since I arrived in Montverrier. His eyes brimmed with joy; his mouth was a wide, heart-stopping flash of white teeth in the gloomy station.

'I have my motorbike outside,' he said. 'May I give you a lift?'

I nodded, and he reached out a hand, sweeping me up with him onto my feet and into the strong clasp of his arms.

His eyes danced as he looked down at me.

'A dinner of steak and red wine.'

'A meal fit for a princess.' I laughed up at him and took his hand in mine.

And so we made our way out of the station and into the golden

Mediterranean sun, leaving the principality of Montverrier, and all its lies and secrets, far behind us.